ANCIENT ADVENTURES

COUNTY DURHAM & NORTHUMBERLAND TALES

Edited By Emily Wilson

Years of

First published in Great Britain in 2017 by:

YoungWriters

Coltsfoot Drive
Peterborough
PE2 9BF
Telephone: 01733 890066
Website: www.youngwriters.co.uk

FOREWORD

Welcome to 'Ancient Adventures - County Durham & Northumberland Tales'.

Young Writers' latest competition was 'Ancient Adventures' which involved writing a 100 word historical mini saga about something, you guessed it, historical. By far the most popular time period this collection was ancient Egypt so you will encounter lots of mummies, pharaohs, tomb robbers and even Howard Carter. The Second World War was also a popular theme so there some very interesting stories about the battlefield as well as the home front – but whatever time period is your favourite, I'm sure there is a story in here for you.

We had a great response to this competition and the entries came storming in! All the work we received was great fun to read – it's always great to see which aspects of history capture your imaginations and what adventures you can create. The standard was very high and I would like to say a huge thank you to everyone who sent in a mini saga for our competition. I hope seeing your work published inspires you to keep writing and maybe I'll come across some more of your tales in our future competitions.

Now let's take a step back in time and see what adventures await us in this collection.

Emily Wilson

CONTENTS

Fens Primary School, Hartlepool

Jasmine Stabler (10)	53
Mia Grace Brown (10)	54
Emily Hall (10)	55
Sophia Fenwick (9)	56
Grace Kelly (11)	57
Jessica Charlton (11)	58
Lorena Andrews (10)	59
Alysia Lakin (10)	60

Peases West Primary School, Crook

Sophie Walton (11)	61
Caitlin Genner (11)	62
Libby Thompson (11)	63
Alannah Wheatley (11)	64
Ellie Brown (11)	65
Rachelle Pratt (10)	66

St Patrick's RC Primary School, Stanley

Ben Walsh (10)	67
Te'kiah Smiely (9)	68
Jon Young (10)	69
Jack Edgar (10)	70
William Mayo (9)	71
Martha Carr (9)	72
Esmé-Niamh Isles (10)	73
Abbie Newstead (9)	74
Harry Grundy (10)	75
Uzziel Smily (9)	76
Kara Drummond (10)	77
Olivia Morris (9)	78
Aaron Jamie Steven Taylor (10)	79
Charlie Whittaker (10)	80
Lucy Peart (9)	81
Kyle Fazakerley (9)	82

Thomas Young (10)	83
Jennifer Ross (9)	84
Rhys Charlton (8)	85
Cameron Hoskin (10)	86
Abigail Robson (9)	87
Emily Williamson (10)	88
Seon Wilson (9)	89
Tom Edgar (10)	90
Cameron Newbould (9)	91
Charlotte Fraser (9)	92
Danny Noble (9)	93
Joshua Stephenson (10)	94
Rhys Mosey (9)	95
Archie Berry (9)	96
Rhys Warner (9)	97

Sugar Hill Primary School, Newton Aycliffe

Ryan Downton (7)	98
Emma Danby (10)	99
Cameron Bell (9)	100
Liam Gibson (9)	101
Lucy Brooks (9)	102
Cameron Mansur Sevim (9)	103
Josie Thompson (8)	104
Shae Rowland (10)	105
Owen Gressmann (9)	106
Jessica Burnside (9)	107
Ebony Thompson (10)	108
Poppy Hobson (8)	109
Jude Hoar (10)	110
Ruby Amelia Hindmarch (8)	111
Harry Laight (9)	112
Jasmine Hope (9)	113
William Hall (10)	114
Conner James Bennett (10)	115
Morgan Mason (9)	116
Erin Russell (9)	117
Moore Swainston (7)	118
Anthony Gowland (9)	119

Alyisha Patton (9)	120
Lexie Duffy (8)	121
Harvey Yale (8)	122
Lauren Kavanagh (8)	123
Tyler Cunliffe (9)	124
Jack Surman (10)	125
Layton Collier Grant (8)	126
Lucy Grayson (9)	127
Tyler Gibbon (9)	128
Ellie Davies (9)	129
Grace Buck (9)	130
Amy Richardson (8)	131
Anna Wren (9)	132
Sophie Grace Evans (9)	133
Callum McBride (9)	134
Keira Richardson (9)	135
Alfie Land (8)	136
Sophie Flint (9)	137
Joe Wren (8)	138
Oliver Paylor (8)	139
Isaac Taylor (9)	140
Ruby Hancock (8)	141
Chloe Heslop (9)	142
Rhys Galloway (9)	143
Liam Bell (9)	144
Thomas Aspinall (9)	145
Harry Surman (8)	146
Michael Pritchard (9)	147
Teegan Briscoe (8)	148
Gracie-Mai Cowper (8)	149
Sophie M (9)	150
James Behan (9)	151
Lincoln Hudson (8)	152
Ryan Foreman (9)	153
Ellie Horner (7)	154
Lydia Deboer (8)	155
Emma Ainsworth (10)	156

THE
MINI SAGAS

Manic Mummy

'Wow!' exclaimed the explorer looking around at the spectacular pyramids. *Smash! What was that?* she thought. She turned the corner into a room, she saw the beautiful Cleopatra mummifying someone. All of a sudden the mummy jumped up.

'Argh!' screamed Cleopatra, as it started chasing them down the stairs, along the corridor and out the door. Outside there was a terrible roaring sandstorm.

'Over here!' shouted Cleopatra. She led them to her palace.

'I have an idea,' said Becky the explorer. Back outside they went and they pulled hard on the cloth of the mummy and it vanished.

Isabel Hughes (10)
Abbey Junior School, Darlington

The WWII Battle

'It's a long way to Tipperary...' everyone continued.
'It's getting hot!' I said to myself.
'Only a thousand miles to go!' whispered a voice behind me. When we did eventually get there we met the other enemy.
After about ten days, during the night, we were in the bunker and eating and chatting quietly. The next day we all were attacking when suddenly all the enemies ran back. Everyone was saying, 'We have won!' and then out of the beautiful sparkly blue sky a gigantic bomb hit and killed a lot of people, but in the end we won.

William Watson (10)
Abbey Junior School, Darlington

Mummy Loose In Egypt

I go down to an ancient tomb and I hear a noise. It's footsteps. It's a mummy! I run to Cleopatra's palace (it's huge!) I tell her about the mummy but she doesn't believe me. I say, 'If I bring it to you, then will you believe me?'
'OK, but be gone now.'
A boy runs up to me called Tomeus and says, 'I'll help!' So we go to the dark tomb again. But the mummy isn't there. We run to the palace to tell Cleopatra but she says, 'A mummy loose in Egypt? What? How did this happen?'

Issy Laver (10)
Abbey Junior School, Darlington

World War 2

One day a little girl called Anne lived in a nice house with a really nice family. One day people from the war knocked on the door and told the whole family that they had to go to the concentration camp.

Once they got to the camp they all got a gas mask. It would be three years until they could go back home.

Three years had passed and all of the family could go home. When they got back their home had fallen down. But Anne and the family had money to buy a house. They lived happily ever after.

Ruby Clarkson (10)
Abbey Junior School, Darlington

The Gruesome Execution

Once there was a man called Henry. Henry was King of England and he was evil. He was going to chop off Steve, King of Sweden's head for coming to England.

'Steve your execution is ready!' said the guard. Steve was taken for his execution, trembling with nerves. Crowds were booing as King Steve of Sweden came out to the crowds chanting, 'Execution, execution, execution.' The executioner was ready, three, two, one, *Chop!* The head was off. The public crowds roared with cheer as they thought England was the greatest.

William Gray (10)
Abbey Junior School, Darlington

Mummy On The Loose

'Wow look at this,' I said to Margot my dog. It was a coffin, it was empty but it looked like we had disturbed someone. We turned, and right before my very eyes it was a mummy! We ran and ran and ran, if we did stop I wouldn't like to see what happened! There were lots of booby-traps. I think Margot just missed one. I pushed down a coffin, Margot jumped over and the mummy fell in. I shut the lid, we heard it wailing. 'That was hard wasn't it?'
Margot agreed with me.

Kit Hodgson (9)
Abbey Junior School, Darlington

The Mummies Nightmare

One day deep in the tomb there were mummies and pharaohs celebrating the Ceremony of the Dead. Osiris was reading from the Book of the Dead as usual and then they heard a sound. The mummies were murmuring, wondering what the suspicious noise of clicking was and in the room came humans! The humans ran and screamed and the mummies chased. They had already run through five tombs when the mummies caught up and brought them back and kept them imprisoned. It was a little while before they were let out, when that happened they bit the humans! Mummies!

Joseph Fields (10)
Abbey Junior School, Darlington

World War 2 - The Jew

I stared at him with hatred, his eyes darted through my heart. Holding tightly to my star. They're packing Jews on carts. I miss home, I miss dad. I wish we could be the same as everyone I wish nobody would hurt me, we got there, eventually. Everyone's Jewish, nobody's happy, everyone is slim and pale. We had a mattress to share with five people. Today was hard work. I cried myself through it. Mum stood up for us, they killed her. I feel trapped, I am trapped. I'll fight through this and I won't just survive, I'll win.

Charlotte Rayner (10)
Abbey Junior School, Darlington

Jane Seymour's Execution

Once there was a king named Henry VIII and he had loads of wives. So he married his third wife Jane Seymour, but she didn't want to marry somebody who was married before, but King Henry liked her so he lied. Jane Seymour was suspicious because he already had dresses and girly stuff. So Jane Seymour decided to send some people to spy on him. When King Henry was in his bedroom, the spy saw him planning a funeral for his second wife Anne Boleyn. He told Jane Seymour and she got his head chopped with a axe. *Chop!*

Fateema Bawarish (10)
Abbey Junior School, Darlington

World War II On The Train

One day there was a war going on. Emily and William were getting ready to go on the train. The screaming and shouting was really loud. We got on the train and all the carriages were full so we went in a carriage with two boys called Kit and Sam. We were about halfway into the journey when Kit and Sam suddenly disappeared. Emily looked surprised. William looked at Emily. Then suddenly the train stopped. The door opened and Sam and Kit sat down again like nothing had happened. They were ghosts not ordinary people like me or you!

Emily Robson (9)
Abbey Junior School, Darlington

Bombed!

It was World War Two. A family was having a picnic at Green Park. The mum was pregnant and she had with her two little girls. One of her daughters was called Poppy, she was seven, the other was called Anna, she was eleven. When they were eating there was a loud whistle of a bomb. There were no bomb shelters around. The closest thing to a shelter was a hole. Suddenly the mum screamed, she was giving birth. The bomb hit, but only the baby survived and to this day no one knows what happened to his family, only the bomber knows.

Alex Payne (10)
Abbey Junior School, Darlington

The Dark Depths

I was walking in the deep depths of the desert. The sound of my feet echoed round the tomb. I held a torch high above me. *Thud!* I turned round. I squinted at the dark around me. Nothing. I took a step back. I felt something behind me. I turned round slowly and right there was a mummy! I ran. It lumbered after me. I came to a dead end. It came closer and closer towards me. I leant back and... fell. Down, down, down, I could hear the mummy following in pursuit. *Bang, thud!* And then I woke up!

Isabella Tait (9)
Abbey Junior School, Darlington

World War II - The Blitz

I was walking up the stairs getting ready for bed, I got into bed and fell asleep straight away. Before I knew it my brother was shaking me awake. As soon as I got up I heard the siren. I was terrified. I sprinted outside and dived into the small air raid shelter. Once we were all in I slammed the door shut. I got into bed and fell asleep. I woke up in the night because of a loud bang. I thought it was something falling then I realised it was a bomb. I woke up, everything was smashed.

Dylan Wilson (10)
Abbey Junior School, Darlington

Cavemen

There was once an orphan boy named Benny and the only toy he had was a dinosaur, he wanted to meet one someday. It was bedtime, but he woke up in a cave entrance. Then he found himself in the cave and was searching for dinosaurs. But when he got to the cave's end, he found unusual men... Cavemen! They were making weird noises. He told them he was an orphan and they said that they would look after him but he was trapped! So he lived with them forever more.

Nina Sutherland (10)
Abbey Junior School, Darlington

The Greek Gods

One sunny day Hades was in the underworld patting his three headed dog called Cerberus. Just then Zeus appeared right in front of him, 'What do you want?' demanded Hades.

'I want you to see Poseidon,' said Zeus.

Two minutes later Hades and Poseidon were standing next to each other.

'Fight!' shouted Zeus.

So Poseidon smacked his trident against Hades' sword but Hades used all his strength and beat Poseidon to the floor of the underworld. 'OK you win,' Poseidon said angrily.

Poseidon stormed off to Athens. Then Cerberus and Hades turned into ghosts and floated back to Mount Olympus.

Ethan Taylor (7)
Abbeyfields First School, Morpeth

Theseus And The Minotaur

Long ago there was an island called Athens. Every nine years seven girls and seven boys had to go to Crete and face the Minotaur or they declared war on Athens. King Minos had a daughter called Ariadne.

One year Theseus told his father that he was going to slay the beast. 'No, don't go!' begged his father. 'I have no choice,' said Theseus.

'Okay but if you kill the beast, come back with a white sail.'

Theseus battled with the Minotaur and defeated it. He escaped the labyrinth with the help of Ariadne who gave him the string.

Oliver Armstrong (8)
Abbeyfields First School, Morpeth

Baby Athena

One day Zeus had a horrible headache 'My head, my head,' cried Zeus.

The next day Zeus told Hera about the headache and Heparstus and Ares both heard and the boys bounded into Zeus and Hera's room. 'What's happened to Daddy's head?' asked Ares.

'He's just got a bit of a headache,' answered Hera.

One week passed and two legs were sticking out of Zeus's head. The next week there were arms as well. Finally after two weeks the baby popped out. *Pop!* It was a little girl fully dressed in armour with a shield and Zeus called her Athena.

Teddy Davidson (8)
Abbeyfields First School, Morpeth

Queen Victoria's Bad Day

Queen Victoria woke up to a grey, gloomy day. She rang her bell and a servant girl brought her breakfast. 'I'll go and wake the children,' she sighed, so off she went. She came back two minutes later, screaming 'My soap is gone.'
'Right children, who did this?' she demanded, but nobody came.
Next she found her cape was ripped! She didn't call the boys though. Next she found her best shoes were lost and jewels from her crown were lost. The boys made a booby trap with ink as well. She got very mad, *I hate my children*!'

Libby Shooter (8)
Abbeyfields First School, Morpeth

Our World War II

We were going to war with Germany. I was a pilot for the Royal Air Force. One day the Germans started bombing London! 'Get in your planes,' said Fin.

So Ed and me jumped in our Spitfires, 'Come on Red Squadron, let's knock out these Germans,' I said.

The leader for the German Luftwaffe was known for his fearsome battling. Our enemy. I was flying through the sky shooting at the Germans, suddenly I saw the Luftwaffe leader. I knew what I had to do so I looped the loop and shot him down. Luckily we would live another day, 'Hot digity dog!'

Tom Gibson (8)
Abbeyfields First School, Morpeth

The Big Fight

Once there was a rightful ruler called Zeus, he had two brothers called Poseidon and Hades, his wife is called Hera. Hephaestus is his oldest child.

One day Hera and Zeus were shouting at each other, they were kicking each other by the time it was dark.

In the morning they got even worse, they were kicking, punching and nipping each other. They went to a posh restaurant and still they were fighting. Suddenly Hephaestus stopped the fight because he was fed up. That night they separated and got divorced, and went to live on different sides of Greece.

Tara Twynholm (8)
Abbeyfields First School, Morpeth

The Story Of World War 2

One day a girl called Molly was packing, she was getting ready to leave her family. It was 1939 and she was being evacuated to the countryside where it was safe from the bombs. Her mother was taking her to the train station where she met the other children.

'Bye Mother,' she shouted, whilst getting on the train.

On the train she met some people called Lilly and Charlie, they were twins. When Molly got off the train, her Auntie Greta and Uncle James were there. After two long years her mother came back for her. She was so happy.

Eden Rose Armit (8)
Abbeyfields First School, Morpeth

Medusa And The Ten Men

One Halloween night was freaking people out because it was the day when Medusa struck. Ten men came racing into the woods where Medusa lived. 'Help us,' said a man to Athena up in the sky. Medusa came out and looked a man straight in his eyes. He turned to stone. Eight of the men ran away but one man named Perseus stayed, he was going to kill Medusa. Medusa hid behind a tree and then jumped out. Athena helped Perseus by casting a spell on Medusa. Perseus cut off Medusa's head and her body fell to the floor. Yucky!

Riley Chivers (8)
Abbeyfields First School, Morpeth

The Bombers Are Coming

One sunny day there was a familiar sound in the air. It was bombers and lots of them. 'Get in the air,' called Hugo.

They were in the air in a flash! In seconds they destroyed the first two bombers and the third, then the fourth. They went down like dominoes. They came to the last three bombers, 'Finn and Tom take the one on the left and Ed and Fred take the one on the right.' They all followed their instructions and within a few minutes the rest of the bombers were shot down. The mission was a success.

Huw Laude (8)
Abbeyfields First School, Morpeth

Perseus And Medusa

Once there was a man called Perseus who wanted to slay a Gorgon called Medusa. The only problem was she lived in a cave in an unknown place, but he still went.

Finally he got there, he had his sword and shield at the ready. He hid behind a rock, then he popped up and sliced off Medusa's head and put it in the bag. He ran as fast as he could back home and then became really famous in his town soon in his whole country! So he lived like a celebrity forever more in a large, beautiful palace.

Morgan Collings (8)
Abbeyfields First School, Morpeth

Athena Changing Medusa Into A Gorgon

By the river there was Athena and Medusa sitting together. Medusa was admiring herself in Athena's shield, Athena said, 'You really are pretty.' Then Poseidon came up and got angry with Medusa because Athena had called Medusa really pretty and he thought his daughters were prettier than her. Then Athena had to fight off her own uncle, Poseidon, which made her angry too so she stabbed Medusa with her magic sword which turned her into a Gorgon. That Gorgon could turn you to stone because she was so ugly now. Then later that Gorgon Medusa got her head chopped off!

Eve Hendy (8)
Abbeyfields First School, Morpeth

About A Boy Called Theseus

A long time ago there was a boy called Theseus and in these ancient times there was a Minotaur. Theseus dared himself to fight the Minotaur, his dad really didn't want him to go in case he died. Ariadne gave Theseus a ball of string to help him find his way out of the labyrinth. Theseus entered the labyrinth and there he found the Minotaur. Theseus killed it and escaped. Sadly King Minos threw himself off a cliff because he thought Theseus was dead. Theseus desperately searched for his father, he was devastated by his death but became king.

Jack Dunn (8)
Abbeyfields First School, Morpeth

Goddess Of War

Once there was a God called Zeus. He was the rightful ruler. Then one day Zeus had a headache it was really annoying, then suddenly... a girl popped out of his head! She was all dressed in armour with a spear on her back. It had a lovely diamond on it. She could also magically turn a person into a terrifying mythical monster. Zeus' brother Poseidon wanted to challenge her, so Athena gave a big olive tree. He was amazed at this however his brother caused a flood of salty water so Zeus was furious with him. Athena won.

Molly Willis (8)
Abbeyfields First School, Morpeth

Theseus And The Minotaur

It was a windy day and it was the day before the big battle. Everybody was getting ready. They put their helmets and armour on. They thought it would be the best battle ever. However Theseus and Hercules had a task to do first, they had to kill the Minotaur. Theseus was going first. Hercules gave him string to find his way out so he went in and straight away he killed the creature. However they didn't realise that they'd missed the battle; it was a tricky battle, some people hid but they won the battle anyway.

Jack Featherstone (8)
Abbeyfields First School, Morpeth

World War I

In the first World War there were two friends, Ben and Alan. They were fighting against Germany. The Germans had more men than the English. However the Germans could still lose. The two friends had guns, Alan had a machine-gun, Ben had a rifle. They were trapped but they had a plan. The Germans went to the first squad and in the meantime the English killed all of the Germans, but a German killed Ben. Alan was really angry so he killed a lot of Germans. England had one thousand men and Germany had a few.

Cameron Douglas (8)
Abbeyfields First School, Morpeth

Theseus And The Minotaur

Once there was a young man called Theseus. He lived in Athens. One day, he went to Crete where he met King Minos, owner of the Minotaur. Theseus went in the labyrinth. He went forwards then backwards as he missed a turn off. He turned right, then left, then right again. Eventually, he found the Minotaur in the centre of the huge maze. He twisted its head all the way around. It was dead and blood was rolling around the floor. Theseus brought its skull home.

Rosie Yates (8)
Abbeyfields First School, Morpeth

The Explorer And The Glowing Clock

One morning Jess was walking around the museum and the clock struck ten. Suddenly, Jess saw a light coming from the clock. Then everything turned purple. She was being sucked into the dock! *Whoosh!* She was flying off. Suddenly, she found herself in the mountains, 'Whoa! What? Where am I? I'm in the middle of nowhere,' said Jess. Then she saw a T-rex! 'Oh now I know where I am... The dinosaur age!' said Jess.

'What is this?' said Jess as she picked something up, 'Ew it's dry dinosaur poo,' said Jess. It was time for her to go.

Katherine Keech (9)
Bothal Primary School, Ashington

The Queen's Throne

Once upon a time there was a queen called Lilly Brennan, she wanted to rule her sister's throne. Lilly wanted the throne really badly, she rang her sister and said, 'If you don't give me the throne, you'll die!'
Her sister was offended, she didn't know what to do so she gave her throne to her sister. Lilly ruled the kingdom. She was so glad.

Lilly Michelle Brennan (10)
Bothal Primary School, Ashington

The Unknown Island!

One dull, foggy day, I was looking for land to settle in, when I saw this ancient monastery that looked like it had treasure in it. Since I was the captain, I shouted, 'Charge!' and pointed my sword at the small island, my longship turned towards the island. My hair blew behind me, I was a really proud captain! When we arrived the monks were standing there ready, I didn't care, we killed most of them and stole the monastery's treasure. When we'd pretty much taken over, we saw another island, but it was enormous, way bigger than Holy Island...

Eva Wakenshaw (9)
Bothal Primary School, Ashington

Jeff The Viking And The Weird Portal

One day there live a Viking named Jeff. He absolutely loved portals. Jeff had a mum called Eva and a dad called Eric. Jeff had a friend called Jack. Jeff and Jack found out about a new portal so they made it and went through. When they got there, there were dinosaurs everywhere so Jeff and Jack ran rapidly away from the dinosaurs. When they stopped they realised they didn't have a clue where the portal was! They walked and walked and finally found the portal. So they went through and told Jeff's parents all about their amazing portal journey!

Erin Johnson (9)
Bothal Primary School, Ashington

The Voice From The Grave

The gloomy trees swayed in the wind as I looked at Granny's grave. I heard a whisper. It said, 'Ben.' I started to investigate as another voice came. It was the gravedigger. I run as it started to thunder. *Grrr*, I heard something. As I get closer I can make out shadows. I gasp, there before my very eyes are zombies and ghosts. They all turn their beady eyes on me and I start to run. In the distance I see lights. At first they're scary, but when I realise it's just the gravedigger coming for me, I'm relieved.

Carly Haefner (9)
Bothal Primary School, Ashington

Julie And The Viking

'Argh!' Julie screamed. The vicious Viking warrior ran towards her, yelling at the top of his voice. Julie ran. She picked up some stones and threw them as she fought for her life. The scary warrior searched for her because she had hidden in a nearby cave. Julie had found a sharp knife on the ground and threw it as hard as she could at the Viking. It bounced off his helmet. He headed towards her, 'Help me,' she shouted. The dagger came towards her like a bullet. The Viking had defeated her for good. She had met her doom.

Lorien Dodds-Crouth (9)
Bothal Primary School, Ashington

The Demon Queen

One cold dark night, Queen Elizabeth got bitten by a venomous snake. The snake turned her into a demon. Queen Elizabeth went on a killing spree. The demonic queen could not be caught by anyone! Even the police. One stormy night in Windsor Castle, Harry the servant was giving King Henry a cup of tea. When all of a sudden the queen came out of nowhere! Harry had a potion to cure the queen. Quickly she came and pounced violently onto Harry. He came face with her and swiftly threw the potion onto her and she was cured.

Harry Redshaw (9)
Bothal Primary School, Ashington

A New Life

Rory Madin was not a very good sailor. He had been sick for the full journey so far the Viking longboat had arrived on the Northumberland Coast. Rory and Frode, his brother spent every day working in the fields. They planted many things so they would always have something to eat. Night-time was scary but they had each other and felt safe in the long house they built together. It was made of wood, sticks and mud. It kept them dry and it kept the animals dry as well. This new life was brilliant.

Robbie Martin (9)
Bothal Primary School, Ashington

The Workhouse

I'm a Victorian boy living in the streets of Newcastle. The streets are covered in poo and wee. I have no mum or dad, as they died when I was young. I think they died of smallpox. I am looking for food and a place to sleep. I've not eaten since Friday, it is now Sunday. I might have to do the thing I have always feared, going to the workhouse! I walk down the lonely dark street. It's scary for a seven-year-old boy. I made the decision I have to knock on that dark, gloomy door!

William Oliver Brown (9)
Bothal Primary School, Ashington

Roman Rampage

When I was in Italy, some Romans captured me. I realised it was Julius Caesar. They took me to Rome. Then he threw me in a cage full of lions. There were crowds of people in the empire. Five lions versus one person. I defeated the lions. He was so angry he tried to chop my head off, luckily I grabbed the sword and chopped his head off. I became the Roman Emperor. I was happy for the rest of my life. It was the best holiday ever. I never told anybody else. So I kept the secret to myself.

Rhys Gill (9)
Bothal Primary School, Ashington

Innocent

'Andierous Balshaw, you're accused of killing your father,' exclaimed the tribe leader. Cowering down, Andierous listened to him, 'You'll be thrown in a river, a sack of venomous snakes on your back.' If he survived he was innocent but if he drowned he was guilty.

Later that evening, Andierious prayed that he would survive, as he was thrown in the currents, gasping for air, he desperately pulled his way through the fast-flowing tide. Finally, he reached the riverbank. Despite the fact everyone thought he was guilty, Andierous was an innocent man. Who was the criminal? What would he do next?

Keira Jones (10) & Carys Plews (11)
Cockton Hill Junior School, Bishop Auckland

Killer Mummy

Peering around the mysterious tomb Howard Carter found an ancient sarcophagus. Covering the beautiful coffin were bright blue and gold gems that sparkled in the sun light.

'This is an outstanding discovery,' shouted Howard to himself. In the distance Howard Carter spotted some amazing treasure. However, out of the corner of his eye he could see a mummy coming towards him. Running around the large room, Howard suddenly came to a dead end. The mummy got closer and closer... Unravelling one of his bandages the creature wrapped it around Howard Carter's nose and mouth. Was this the end of him?

Corvin Burke (11)
Cockton Hill Junior School, Bishop Auckland

Unexpected

Two girls waited nervously for King Tut to arrive not knowing that he didn't want visitors. Murderously, staring at each other, the two girls knew they were both here to meet the king - Cleo couldn't let that happen. Cleo threw the first move. Bashing Nefertiti's head into the crusted wall, she collapsed to the ground and lay there lifeless while her head spilled with ruby blood. Cleo, who was feeling strong, paced into the pyramid to find something she didn't expect... Nails pierced her soft, silky skin as she plummeted downwards. Proudly King Tut stood and exclaimed, 'Nailed it!'

Sophie Appleton (11)
Cockton Hill Junior School, Bishop Auckland

Don't Forget Your Head!

Storming down to the misty dungeons, Henry and Anne wanted to inspect what was inside. Covering the rusty walls, were delicate spiderwebs and a dead rat lay on the kitchen floor. Marching in the evil guard shouted, 'We're ready!' Henry mumbled, 'Leave her to me. She'll be absolutely fine!' Wearing a magnificent belt. Henry drew out a terrifying axe. Henry viciously flicked his strong hand and Anne's disgusting head started to roll on the stone cold floor. Mischievously strolling out like nothing had happened, King Henry was proud of himself for chopping off Anne's bloody head.

Sophie Dye (11)
Cockton Hill Junior School, Bishop Auckland

Killer Mummy

Peering around the mysterious tomb Howard found an ancient Sarcophagus. Covering the coffin were blue and gold gems that sparkled in the daylight. 'This is an outstanding discovery,' shouted Howard. Suddenly he spotted lots of different treasure. There were many things: silver necklaces, blue diamonds and golden rings. Out of the corner of his blue eyes, he could see something. It was a mummy... Running around the tomb Howard came to a dead end and the mummy got closer and closer, revealing one of his bandages, the mummy wrapped it around Howard's nose and mouth. Was this the end?

Jon-Joe Bolton (11)
Cockton Hill Junior School, Bishop Auckland

She Sat On The Bus

Rosa sat on the bus as she had done everyday for the past year. However, today was different. She paid for her ticket, but today she sat at the front among the white people, instead of with the black people at the back. Immediately, the bus driver demanded she move, but something triggered in her mind... Racism wasn't right! Within seconds, the police arrived. Rosa didn't budge. Desperately trying her hardest to remain seated, Rosa felt vulnerable and scared as the police dragged her from the bus. Rosa is still remembered today for her amazing work and dedication against racism.

Sienna Denham (10)
Cockton Hill Junior School, Bishop Auckland

The Roman Battle

A brave Roman soldier on a battlefield waited nervously for the battle to commence. Blood curdling cries echoed all around the soldiers. Bodies dropped like flies everywhere on the blood soaked battlefield. Swords were clashing and time appeared to stand still. The battlefield was full of wounded and dead soldiers. The battle was over. A sigh of relief was heard coming from the brave surviving soldiers. One of the Roman soldiers knelt on the ground to thank God for keeping him alive against his dark enemies. And they never fought against their enemies again. They were thankful.

Leon Ellsworth (11)
Cockton Hill Junior School, Bishop Auckland

Booby Traps Attack

Surrounded by ancient walls, the archaeologist, Howard Carter huddled up to Cleopatra's treasure. All of a sudden, another treasure hunter slowly approached. He was called Jeff. He put up a fight for the treasure, as fast as a cheetah, Howard pushed Jeff onto a booby-trap and part of the ceiling collapsed on him! Sadly he died. Nervously Howard opened the sarcophagus and a mummy pounced out at him. Sprinting like lightning to the entrance of the tomb, Howard saw the doorway crumble to the floor. With a loud scream, Howard was eaten by the mummy. They were never seen again.

Sam Guy (11)
Cockton Hill Junior School, Bishop Auckland

Tutankhamun Awakens

In the depths of modern Egypt Tutankhamun awakened. Leaving his ancient, fancy tomb, he noticed Egypt was completely different. Quickly running towards his golden throne, Tutankhamun wanted to become pharaoh again. When he arrived he was amazed: he'd forgotten how fantastic the great palace was. However as soon as he arrived he spied the wonderful throne. As quick as a flash he stole a dagger and challenged the new pharaoh to a fight. Sword fighting to the death the current pharaoh was too strong and he cut Tutankhamun's head off! A story to go down in future history.

Charlie Crinion (11)
Cockton Hill Junior School, Bishop Auckland

Death In Paradise!

Crystal jewels and precious diamonds surrounded Howard Carter and his team in the tomb. Looking into the distance, a shining light appeared. As they edged towards the light, skulls hung from the stone roof and rotten flesh was being eaten by flea-ridden rats. Nervously walking across the abandoned room. Howard was struck with fear as dark shadows appeared. Screams filled the air as Howard's team were vanishing one by one. As he reached the end of the room, a golden crown was placed on a throne. Dashing with the crown looking for a escape a figure appeared. Was this it?

Brandan Woods (11)
Cockton Hill Junior School, Bishop Auckland

Trapped Forever

Surrounded by ancient walls, was Harold, a treasure hunter looking around in a temple for loot. Suddenly he spotted something sparkling in the distance and walked towards it. When he got closer, he realised it was an old dusty tomb with gold and jewels in it. As he slowly opened it, he grabbed all of the treasure and put it in his backpack. All of a sudden, a mummy appeared out of nowhere, in the darkness and started to chase him into a trap which made rocks fall over the entrance. He got eaten. He was never seen again.

Louis Moore (11)
Cockton Hill Junior School, Bishop Auckland

The Jurassic Game

After being sucked into a video game, I was stood in the middle of a mysterious forest, not knowing how to get out. Nestled in the middle of the jungle I heard ferocious footsteps. It was a dinosaur... Crimson scales coated its large body like armour. Petrified I ran for my life. Suddenly I came to a dead end. We were face to face and I was an inch away from death. However, without warning I fell straight back into the present and completed the adventurous game with a glowing smile on my face.

Megan Ellison (11)
Cockton Hill Junior School, Bishop Auckland

Cheater!

Dear Diary,

Today was an amazing day for me, here's why. Early hours this morning I snuck into Catherine's room and cautiously manoeuvred her down into the chambers. A few hours later Catherine woke up to a crowd of people surrounding her, laughing. I explained to her how I found out she was cheating on me with my closest and best servant Thomas Culpeper. Three... two... one... *splat!* The blade sliced through her neck as the crowd went wild. I chuckled with joy as her parents confronted me and yelled, 'You monster!' and stormed upstairs in tears feeling devastated.

Jasmine Stabler (10)
Fens Primary School, Hartlepool

Meeting Henry By Anne Of Cleves

I stepped out of my magnificent carriage, my emerald green gown sparkling in the sun. I couldn't wait to see Henry. I was shown to the courtyard where music deafened me. *It couldn't be happening,* I thought, *this is a dream.* Suddenly, a cloaked figure tapped my shoulder unexpectedly. I looked around but Henry wasn't there. The figure grabbed me and I screamed. *Was he going to try and kiss me?* I thought. The crowds gasped as I ran away, tears rolling down my bloodshot eyes. 'Henry?' I whispered. But obviously I got no reply, where on earth was he?

Mia Grace Brown (10)
Fens Primary School, Hartlepool

The Heads

One fine morning Hercules happened to be strolling up Mount Olympus when... Oh uh, Hydra! *Roar!* The noise banged on Hercules' ear drums like a big brass band. *Chop,* a head was sliced clean off! Suddenly, two more grew back! The hero had made a bet with the king that he had to bring a head back to him, otherwise he would lose his. *Plunge,* the beast had been stabbed! Its heads flailed around. *Poof!* They all hit the ground. The king now had his trophy, all thanks to Hydra. All he had to say was three little words: 'Thank you Father!'

Emily Hall (10)
Fens Primary School, Hartlepool

The Visit!

Henry VIII was getting ready for bed, the window banged against the sill and the curtains billowed wildly in the wind. Henry tried to forget about the uneasy feeling he had. What was going on? Instead of being courageously brave, Henry managed to squeeze one little scream from his trembling mouth. Suddenly, a graceful, hooded figure emerged into view. Henry clambered into his royal bed, tears streaming down his face. The mysterious shadow lowered the cloak, Henry saw that it was Anne Boleyn! 'I thought I killed you last week, why have you come back to haunt me?' stammered Henry.

Sophia Fenwick (9)
Fens Primary School, Hartlepool

The Gorgon Named Medusa

Her beady eyes snarled like an angry scorpion, the hissing of her untamed snakes broke the silence of the midnight sky. Daylight crashed into the area, she woke up one eye then the next, wondering when her first trouble making guest will come. It wasn't long before he arrived armed like never before, his name Theseus. She whipped her long devilish locks back out of her face as she paced along her dark, gloomy cave. Medusa glared straight at him. He instantly froze like his statue followed by his shield crashing to the stone floor! *Crash!*

Grace Kelly (11)
Fens Primary School, Hartlepool

Break In

One dark night, Henry VIII was getting himself ready for bed. He was changing into his nightwear when all of a sudden he heard a rattling noise outside of his chambers. He tried to forget about it but that didn't seem possible. It was starting to unsettle him. Suddenly it got louder and the door hinges started to rattle - somebody was trying to break in! Eventually the door gave way, and a huge man dressed in black robes strolled into the room, took out his sword and pointed it at Henry who was cowering in his bed; 'Mummy, help!'

Jessica Charlton (11)
Fens Primary School, Hartlepool

Jurassic Forest

As I trudged my way through the overgrowth using my machete to move the plants out of my face, I heard a sudden noise that startled me and made me whack my face on a branch. Carefully, I wandered about trying to find out what made the noise. After what seemed like months of searching, I found myself face to face with a disgraceful creature that had blood-red eyes, crimson teeth and a wart on its nose. In minutes, I remembered what this was. It was a dangerous dinosaur. Not any old dangerous dinosaur though, it was a T-rex!

Lorena Andrews (10)
Fens Primary School, Hartlepool

The Curse Of The Mummy

In the murky depths of an ancient neglected tomb, whilst a dim light glowed two embalmers were preparing a body for mummification. One of the embalmers got a hook and put it up the mummy's nose, when he yanked it out, with it was a gloopy brain. Then the body started to move, it sat up and then disappeared as quick as lightning. The embalmers ran as fast as they could. Up ahead there was a chamber they ran into it and could not get out. Years later archaeologists found the bodies of the embalmers still there.

Alysia Lakin (10)
Fens Primary School, Hartlepool

The Stalker

The trees were dancing angrily. I hear footsteps
behind. I run. Then I looked behind, it was
something, someone? I couldn't work out who it
was.

After a while it's still following me. I rang a taxi
driver to pick me up. After five minutes it is here,
when I look inside it was the person that was
following me, but how? When he is behind.

When it struck midnight, I panicked and ran to the
village and there he was cleaning my windows...

Sophie Walton (11)
Peases West Primary School, Crook

It's Here

It was dark in the jungle. The full moon shone through the trees. Sophie and I were scared. We heard a rustle in the trees. 'It's a T-rex,' I said. We hid in the bushes he smelt us. He found us, I screamed. It got Sophie so I ran and got away but I was lost.

'What shall I do?' I said in a whisper. Shattering, shaking leaves surrounded me. I knew he was close so I ran. His teeth were bloody as I ran. I stumbled over a rock and I knew I was doomed for good...

Caitlin Genner (11)
Peases West Primary School, Crook

Fear Of The Unknown

I watched the dark gloomy clouds attentively, as they lurked low to the ground, casting indignant shadows up and down the thick brick walls. I listened to the loud rumble of the aeroplanes, flying high up above, ready to bomb everything in sight. The huge bushes coward away in fear, while the bold trees attempted to flatten and tussle with everything in reach. A cold shiver ran up my spine, as I thought about the unpredictable war. Slowly, a wet tear, filled with sorrow, slashed down my pale worried cheeks. When would war finally stop? When would Father come home?

Libby Thompson (11)
Peases West Primary School, Crook

The Day My Heart Stopped

As the murky clouds devoured the sun, the opposing armies charged towards each other, guns in hand, I remembered passionately kissing my wife farewell, promising her that it all would be over in a few weeks. Only now do I realise how wrong I was! Over the last eight months, I have seen so many abominable things: my brothers killed, neighbours wounded, even my own nineteen year old son taken captive. Infuriated by their memories, I charged into the battle, only to come face-to-face with that monster himself... Hitler. That was when a bullet shot through my heart!

Alannah Wheatley (11)
Peases West Primary School, Crook

The Mysterious Creature

The wind was howling as I was training for the First World War. We were leaving the next day and I needed more training. I was practising shooting targets and moving dolls when I heard loud footsteps banging. I didn't know what to do. I started running round but it caught up to me. We were face to face. It's eyes were filled with hunger. *Oh no,* I thought to myself, *what shall I do?* As I was taking steps back the creature was coming closer. *I am going to get eaten,* I thought, I gulped it came extremely close...

Ellie Brown (11)
Peases West Primary School, Crook

The Princess Battle

The dark night a woman called Queen Victoria was walking across a field. And she bumps into two very handsome men, and both of the men want to be her husband, so they said to her. The two men battled for her, they kicked, they punched everything. Jimmy's heart dropped as he lost he shouted, 'No!' This can't be happening. The next morning Jimmy couldn't wake up because he was dead. But John and Queen Victoria got married and changed their names. They also had a baby girl called Isabella and they lived happily ever after.

Rachelle Pratt (10)
Peases West Primary School, Crook

Ancient Football

It was on a normal day when Pele bumps into
Gullit, Pele says, 'Watch out!'
Gullit said, 'You walked into me!'
'Did I? Well I am sorry,' Pele said.
Then Schmeichel, Kaka said, 'Whoa let's sort this
out on the pitch.'
Gullit said, 'We will make our own team.'
As Gullit and Pele were getting ready the crowd
was cheering. Pele and Gullit stepped out and Pele
had kicked off. Neville and Alves passed it to Pele,
he shoots then he scores. The score was 5-0.
Five years later Pele was in hospital because he
had cancer, sadly he died.

Ben Walsh (10)
St Patrick's RC Primary School, Stanley

The Brave French Army!

In 1914 there was a brave army. They didn't speak our language. That army was called the Brave French Army!

'Soldiers get your weapons out! We've got a battle!' yelled the captain. 'What do you think you're doing?' he asked. 'Get your butts up this second!' Everyone was so tired.

'1, 2, 3, eat your sprouts, 4, 5, 6 spit, them out! 7, 8, 9, get ready on time!' the captain shouted. *Boom!* 'Let's go, go, go, go!'

'We're losing men!' cried one of the soldiers. B*ang!* There was violence covering the bloody war! We lost the battle sadly.

Te'kiah Smiely (9)
St Patrick's RC Primary School, Stanley

Ice Age

Whoosh! The air was bitter and the land was isolated until dawn broke out of the misty grey clouds. A ferocious roar came from the sabertoothed tiger called Scar next door. He strolled down to the frosty water to get a nice cold drink. *Splash!* Out of nowhere came Sara Seacow and to the left of him came Mary the mammoth.

'Scar, over here,' said Mary, 'our homes are going to melt!'

'What?' yelled Scar in worry. Panic everywhere!

'Hop on,' demanded Sara, 'I'll try to get you as far away as possible!' It all melted!

Jon Young (10)
St Patrick's RC Primary School, Stanley

The Ancients Combined For The Beautiful Game!

The ancient Egyptian 'Stars' decided to have a friendly against ancient footballers for next seasons ancient league... the training was terrible, broken legs everywhere! The ancient football team were brilliant, Pele Jr, always on the 'leg-end' of everything. Overhead kicks, scorpion kicks, headers, amazing! What will they do next?
The match started, in the space of five minutes it was 5-0 to our team. Pele-Jr is amazing, how will ancient Egypt win? If other teams come, they can transform into one team. Suddenly, Classic XI came bursting in, so we combined... Goal after goal, we scored (combined-team). We won! Unbelievable!

Jack Edgar (10)
St Patrick's RC Primary School, Stanley

Remember, Remember The Fifth Of November

About one hundred years ago, Guy Fawkes was in prison. Suddenly Guy's friends burst through the wall and asked, 'You ready yet mate?'
Guy jumped out of his cell and exclaimed, 'What do you think?' So they set off with their jingling boots. When the prison guard walked past he smelt smoke and fire, he came running and checked on Guy's cell. There was no sign of Guy, just a broken cell. Finally Guy met his best friend, Gunpowder. Bight lights filled the beautiful parliament. The next thing Guy saw was the queen sitting on the seat angrily... Execution.

William Mayo (9)
St Patrick's RC Primary School, Stanley

The Smoke Fills The Air

The smell of smoke, the small sparks. I could see the fire burning everywhere as I was slowly drifting to safety. My house was demolished, my dad and I huddled together. I felt my heart booming like a bomb. I was terrified and my head span around. I thought to myself, *I will I die at the age of nine!* Eventually, I arrived at a new Island it was beautiful, I stood and admired it. But I knew I wouldn't live there.

After three days, the fire stopped and I was able to return home. It was a lucky escape.

Martha Carr (9)
St Patrick's RC Primary School, Stanley

3-2-1 Dodo Birds

The waterfalls were spraying H20. Great, the perfect spot. I dragged my splintered feet to hide. 'Little Dodo bird, come out wherever you are!' cried Monseun the hunter. Monseun was a hard working man with colossal biceps and always has sweat running down his cracked, long nose. No one ever messes with this ten foot man because he always wins. I knew I couldn't hide forever, he will eventually seek me out. I ran. He chased me. Then... Out of nowhere I was dead! My species was extinct!

Esmé-Niamh Isles (10)
St Patrick's RC Primary School, Stanley

The Beast's Awake

The wind howled, leaves rustled around and trees crashed as the monsters approached. All my small ears could hear were loud footsteps coming from outside. I jumped out of my bed, opened the curtains and peeked out my window. My heart froze and stopped and my jaw dropped. There stood the beasts right in front of me. They had bloodied teeth and hunger in their eyes. I sprinted downstairs and closed all of the doors and windows. I was scared to death, so I ran before it engulfed its prey... me. I closed my eyes hoping they would disappear... 'It's a troll!'

Abbie Newstead (9)
St Patrick's RC Primary School, Stanley

Vikings Are Back!

As they were coming towards us it was frightening. On the boat they were all covered in armour and weapons like: sharp swords, deadly pickaxes and a razor-sharp axe. They jumped off the boat and they all roared and smashed the houses with their really dangerous axe. The people which were attacking finished their attack and went away on their wooden boats. They left the land with all the houses wrecked, people injured and some people even died. Thinking they might come again, they made their own army to fight against the terrifying and the fearless Viking warriors.

Harry Grundy (10)
St Patrick's RC Primary School, Stanley

World War II, When Germany Rose

As I heard we had to stay in the shelter. Listening to the dreadful boom and bang. A sizzling round flows out beyond the air. It was a missile, 'My father,' I shouted as the missile targeted directly at him. We were in England. All of the whistling from all of the missiles crashed to the ground. I shivered. The target of Hitler's gun pointed right at me. But we had a missile at his army. So we shot thousands of German soldiers dead right before our feet. We caught Hitler, we asked him questions. 'Shut up, listen.' He didn't so we shot.

Uzziel Smily (9)
St Patrick's RC Primary School, Stanley

The Day The Ash Escaped!

OMG! My life is breaking into pieces, into flames. I can feel in this country that this Mount Vesuvius is going to explode into flames. Hopefully, it will just pass over. This is a dormant volcano, it will never burst out magma. Oh no! It is actually real, it's going to erupt. Everyone will need to pack and run. 'Girls, boys, everyone, pack your bags and go to the other island!' I shouted at them. Nobody listened, everyone ignored me. Then... it happened. It burst into flames! They poured out as fast as a lion. They're scattering all over here!

Kara Drummond (10)
St Patrick's RC Primary School, Stanley

The Great Fire Of London

It started in 1666, in a baker's shop in Pudding Lane close to London Bridge, where they were busy making bread. It was good that the baker's daughter smelt the burning smell. The little girl quickly got out of the house and went to tell her father. Just from a fire in the baker's shop the whole city went up in flames. The great flames set everything on fire, all you could see was smoke. At last on Wednesday the blaze burned itself out. The Great Fire of London destroyed 13,200 houses, 89 churches and 400 streets. Everyone was terrified!

Olivia Morris (9)
St Patrick's RC Primary School, Stanley

Enclosed

I prowled through the pyramid. I was swimming in unchartered waters. My uncle was a wise man. He told me if you're ever in doubt go left, so that's what I did. But Uncle wasn't as 'wise' on this subject; it led me to multiple traps, one of which was a fire! It made me change my undies, it was a bit warm down there! I was too curious to not risk going to jail. Robbery is a big thing nowadays, I could be easily mistaken for committing a crime. But there in front of me lay Tutankhamun's terrifying tomb.

Aaron Jamie Steven Taylor (10)
St Patrick's RC Primary School, Stanley

The Vikings Are Coming

In the distance, a small speck of black floated in the ocean. My brain was very puzzled. It seemed to come closer by the minute. I was still confused. As it came closer, my brain worked harder to figure out what this mysterious object was. Then, I heard, 'Ho ha, ho ha!' Was it the Vikings? I screamed at the top of my voice, 'The Vikings are coming!' Everyone was terrified. The long Viking boat pulled up on the shore. People were still running for cover hoping not to get caught. Pulling the razor blades out, they came to attack.

Charlie Whittaker (10)
St Patrick's RC Primary School, Stanley

Queen Victoria

As I stood there in Buckingham Palace staring at all the expensive, beautiful paintings. Suddenly I heard a voice saying 'What are you doing in here!' I see a head, then a body. I realise it's Queen Victoria. I stood there, frozen, speechless. I knew I should answer her but what could I say. 'Your majesty I didn't realise anyone lived here. I'd better leave.' I realise as I stood there I understood that not everyone is as mean as they look and are in story books. Her earrings were flowers with opals in the middle.

Lucy Peart (9)
St Patrick's RC Primary School, Stanley

Ancient Football And Football Now

Once there was a skillful young man called Legend Pele Jr, who was once playing football for the best team around, Newcastle in the Champions League. They were playing against Sunderland and Newcastle were winning 4-1, Pele Jr scored two and he was running one-on-one about to score a historical hat-trick. But when he was running he ran forward in time to the 2022 World Cup final with England verses Brazil. It was 2-2 and he was taking a penalty and if he scored for England they would win the World Cup. Slowly he ran up and... What a Goal!

Kyle Fazakerley (9)
St Patrick's RC Primary School, Stanley

The End Of The Dinosaurs

One cold night, in the dark Prehistoric world a light glimmered in the vast night. It was getting closer by the hour. Days later, there was a huge ball of fire. The millions of creatures that inhabited this land cowered in fear. They felt defenceless, helpless. The inhabitants that prided themselves on courage lowered their heads in shame, cowards ran to their homes, crying and screaming for help. In mere seconds the creatures would come to a fiery end, the Prehistoric Age was finished. The end of the dinosaurs had come.

Thomas Young (10)
St Patrick's RC Primary School, Stanley

A Peck Of Distance

A time ago before now a mummy was roaming so peacefully in the vast landscape. A blue bandaged mummy was burning in the angry sun. In a basic distance there was only a little peek of golden pyramid so far away from home. Only wishing there was a phone box in the middle of the dry desert. Hoping there was food around. His mouth so dry, his eyes watering from sand. All of a sudden the pyramid turned into a tower. He wished someone owned it. Suddenly a voice said, 'Pizza will be a thrill to have, make it for us.'

Jennifer Ross (9)
St Patrick's RC Primary School, Stanley

The Jurassic Times

He crept to the bones of the stegosaurus, but little did he know that they weren't ordinary bones. Barry went to touch the bones and when he stood back up he noticed he was in a jungle with a real life stegosaurus. Barry ran for his life but he accidentally ran into an angry velociraptor. It was chasing Barry into a dark cave. Barry thought he was safe but when he turned around he saw the beady yellow eyes of the tyrannosaurus rex. Barry sprinted and sprinted with fear when the T-rex ate him. Barry was done for.

Rhys Charlton (8)
St Patrick's RC Primary School, Stanley

Chinese Dragons

The crowd was cheering like a drum. I was thinking will it come? The dragon came out. The dragon was laughing to the ground. The dragon went to the sky, he couldn't believe he could fly. The Chinese dragon had died but he will never be forgotten in the sky. The dragon sighed because he will never die in Beijing where it all began. I bet next year will be a blast but I hope the dragon is OK because if it's not I feel bad. Then I went home sad and felt so bad. This dragon was truly a hero.

Cameron Hoskin (10)
St Patrick's RC Primary School, Stanley

The Midnight Mummy

As I stared at the grave, it looked like it was moving... hang on, it was! A hand covered in tissue was coming out. Soon the whole body was out and very creepy. Worse still it started chasing me. It chased me all around the village. I ran as fast as I could but however fast I ran the mummy was right behind me. As I raced towards the park, I tripped on a fallen tree. I wriggle fiercely but it didn't help. Cold sweat trickled down my back; I realised I was stuck. Just me and the mummy!

Abigail Robson (9)
St Patrick's RC Primary School, Stanley

Pyramid Collapse

The wind howled, trees cracked, loose stones tumbled down onto the rocky sticky floor. As the wind blew I strolled through the storm up to the pyramid. I knocked, *Creak!* While the door opened I stepped back. Wider, wider It opened slowly I walked in. Something came to me I put my hands in front of me. It felt wet, and covered in tissue paper. It came closer so I screamed! I ran but I fell... down a hole I looked up but it was pitch-black and I couldn't see a thing. I lay still I was stuck.

Emily Williamson (10)
St Patrick's RC Primary School, Stanley

Cowboys To The Future!

In the wild west there was a group of cowboys and Indians. The cowboys were chasing the Indians across the beach when a portal appeared and loads of dinosaurs came out of it! One of the monsters was a Megladon, the biggest shark in the world. The shark was chasing them in the water then there was a tyrannosaurus rex so they went so fast that they went into another dimension! It was the World Cup of 2020, but because he couldn't stop he went back to where he had came from, the wild west!

Seon Wilson (9)
St Patrick's RC Primary School, Stanley

Dinosaur Killer

The ground shook and the trees wiggled in the wind as I came face to face with the most eerie beast of all time. I ran and ran and ran as quickly as I could. I didn't even think about breathing as my legs could hardly carry me. I ran through lakes, over mountains, through caves and up trees until I couldn't sprint any more as my legs were too weak to hold me. I fell to the soggy ground and was soon tracked by my latest guest I heard steps and was killed with deadly mortal teeth. I'm dead!

Tom Edgar (10)
St Patrick's RC Primary School, Stanley

Mummy's Terror

As I walked down, the dusty tunnel, I was creeped out by the fading shadows. At that moment I went pale but the weird thing was that it also went really silent. That's when I was face to face with the monster. I shivered in real fear and I did not feel so fragile at that specific moment. In a gentle blink of an eye they were all gone. I thought I was having a vision of a wild dog dragging me to death, but it was all real and the mummy and all his warriors came and killed me.

Cameron Newbould (9)
St Patrick's RC Primary School, Stanley

The Mummy Is Kissing You Good Night

Around 3,000 years ago in the sands of Egypt I was lying down and then... I heard a loud noise coming from the golden temple. I ran to the temple. I looked around but I couldn't see anything at all. But then something moved and then... I went to face my deepest fear. But whatever it was it got away. I sighed in shame. I went to the mummy room. 'One of the mummies is missing!' I yelled. I heard a clatter in the throne room. I ran but it gobbled me up. It was a mummy.

Charlotte Fraser (9)
St Patrick's RC Primary School, Stanley

World War Two Mayhem!

It began on the year 1939 as Hitler bombed English houses. I was dreaming of winning World War Two, but thought it would never happen. I ran. Ran as fast as I could. I heard it chasing me, step by step. I could not go on. I can't feel my legs. I can't feel my body. Then I realised, I had died. Who killed me? What killed me? All I could feel was the bullet in the back of my head. As I collapsed to the ground. I got a glimpse of who killed me. I was killed by Hitler...

Danny Noble (9)
St Patrick's RC Primary School, Stanley

World War 1 Time Travel

One dark and dull morning on the battlefield it was peaceful until the Germans started shooting from the other side of the battlefield. Most of my friends have died but I remain alive. It is just me now in the battle. The Germans were cheating they had a time machine and I went through it... I have finally got to the end and I'm at the battle of the Somme. As the bullets shot over my head, I survived at the end. I was the only survivor...

Joshua Stephenson (10)
St Patrick's RC Primary School, Stanley

Untitled

It was a dark night in the forest. A human was picking strawberries, then all of a sudden he heard a noise, it sounded like footsteps then a mummy kept running but then he ran in the house. Then a lion came in his door but the mummy broke the roof, they caught the man but he escaped. They tried to kill him, he fell but not dead, then got a sword and killed him. They ran away so the human was safe and the lion was never seen again.

Rhys Mosey (9)
St Patrick's RC Primary School, Stanley

The Great Fire Of London

One dark night Mr Farriner was going to bed but Mr Farriner did not put out his fire. While he was sleeping the fire spread further and further onto the street, but no one realised that raging fire was right outside their doors. Finally someone realised that all houses were on fire. Everyone started to scream. Everyone chucked buckets of water on the houses. When the fire stopped Mr Farriner was punished.

Archie Berry (9)
St Patrick's RC Primary School, Stanley

The Terror Of Iceland

The vicious Viking stood right in front of me. He had two wolves with fur blacker than black standing right next to him. My heart came to a complete stop. I held my breath as hard as I could. The howling of the wolves was so deafening that my eardrums almost burst into smithereens. Then all of a sudden the wolves came charging towards me. And at this moment I thought this would be the end of my life. And it was...

Rhys Warner (9)
St Patrick's RC Primary School, Stanley

Scared Of The Mummy

A long time ago in Egypt there was a pharaoh who was having a bath when he heard a strange noise so he got out to take a look and he saw a mummy who was crying.

'What's the matter?' he asked.

'I'm scared of the dark,' said the mummy, 'and I can't sleep because it's dark.'

'I think I have a spare candle you could use,' said the pharaoh.

So he found a candle and helped the mummy light the candle. But the light caught the mummy and set him on fire so sadly the mummy died.

Ryan Downton (7)
Sugar Hill Primary School, Newton Aycliffe

Salina Boo And The Magic Gem

The shining sun slowly rose upon Salina as she strolled along the dusty market with her parents. They slowly turned her by the shoulder and said, 'You're getting married.'
Stumbling backwards Salina shouted, 'No I'm not and you can't make me!'
Leaping through the stalls Salina tripped over a rather small monkey. Salina was about to start yelling but saw something around its neck. It was a tag saying: 'Boo'.
'Guessing that's your name?' said Salina. Boo stepped aside revealing a blue gemstone. She touched it as it started to rain. They smiled at each other dancing in the rain.

Emma Danby (10)
Sugar Hill Primary School, Newton Aycliffe

It Was All A Dream

I was looking around, sightseeing I saw the Roman Empire and the slaves. Suddenly I saw soldiers coming towards me. I said to the soldiers, 'I am very sorry, I was just looking around. I live in England and it is different there!'
The soldiers suddenly grabbed me and pointed their swords at me and said, 'Come with us, you are going to go in the lion's den.'
'I am very sorry, I didn't do anything wrong.'
They were just about to put me in the lion's den and suddenly I woke up!

Cameron Bell (9)
Sugar Hill Primary School, Newton Aycliffe

The First Olympics

Once in ancient Greece the Olympic games began. The first event was javelin and Art was playing. Art came from Canada and he came second.
The next event was the one hundred metre sprint. Eartha was playing and halfway through she fell over. But she carried on and came third winning a bronze medal.
Evan was playing table tennis. He hadn't played that much but he just snuck into second. The last event was archery. Aesop did very well getting bullseye three times and getting a very well deserved gold medal. Eartha came third. Art and Evan got second and Aesop came first.

Liam Gibson (9)
Sugar Hill Primary School, Newton Aycliffe

Kindness In The Life Of A Goddess

One morning Isis was hanging out her washing when she noticed her neighbour, Tefnut crying in the garden. She asked, 'What is wrong?'
She replied, 'My husband is sick and I can't afford food for my children.'
Isis asked Tefnut to come to the fence, hold her hands, and make a wish. Tefnut wished that her husband would get better and she had enough food to feed her children. Suddenly Tefnut heard her husband calling from inside the house, he was putting food out for the family. It was a miracle! From then on they were best friends.

Lucy Brooks (9)
Sugar Hill Primary School, Newton Aycliffe

The Gladiator

The time of the great millennium when great men fought each other in the Colosseum.
All the gladiators had different weapons and awesome names. And the gladiator admired the most was Spartacus. He was big, strong, powerful and brave. You could hear the floor rattle and shake as he stepped in the arena.
The crowd went wild and animals roared. Spartacus fought with honour and courage. All martial skills in kill or be killed. My skin shivered and my eyes filled with pride with blood on his hands dripping he looked up dropped his weapons. He is free!

Cameron Mansur Sevim (9)
Sugar Hill Primary School, Newton Aycliffe

A Titanic Disaster!

As we walked towards the bow of the 'unsinkable ship' we hear a voice scream, 'Iceberg!' Suddenly there is an almighty crash and we fall to the ground. We pick ourselves up and run to the lifeboats, jumping over the chunks of ice which slide across the deck.

'Women and children only,' they shout, as we force our way to the front.

As we are called down into the freezing, dark ocean, we hear the harrowing sound of the bending, twisting hull sailing to safety. We look back on the drowning wreckage of the 'unsinkable ship'!

Josie Thompson (8)
Sugar Hill Primary School, Newton Aycliffe

Tokugawa

Long ago while Japan was at civil war, a boy called Tokugawa was born. Tokugawa was very clever but he was sent away to a rival family as a hostage, 'I miss my family,' cried the boy.
'Shall I teach you how to fight Tokugawa?' The head of his new family offered. Tokugawa wiped his eyes and said, 'Yes, so that I can bring peace to Japan one day.'
He worked hard and gained the biggest army in Japan when he grew up. The emperor then gave Tokugawa control of Japan and brought his country together in peace.

Shae Rowland (10)
Sugar Hill Primary School, Newton Aycliffe

The Pyramid

One night I heard a noise. It woke my friend and I up. We opened our eyes and we were in front of a pyramid, it was ten storeys high, 'Be careful there might be traps in there.'
'OK, do you want to go in there?'
'Yes let's go in.' It was dark, I went through a door, I couldn't see anything, in the distance was a coffin, I opened it, there was a zombie in it. The zombie got up and chased us. I kept running it was fast. I was scared. I got to the wall, it closed.

Owen Gressmann (9)
Sugar Hill Primary School, Newton Aycliffe

Simon's War

One day Simon the Viking meets another Viking called Edward.

Edward only had one tooth and evil eyes that looked right through you. In his hand he had a metal pole with spikes on it, also a wooden shield in his other hand. All of a sudden Edward came charging towards Simon with his weapon held high shouting, 'I am an evil emperor.' Edward started a war against Simon.

Six months later they decided to pack up, move away and never saw each other again.

Jessica Burnside (9)
Sugar Hill Primary School, Newton Aycliffe

The Girl Who Has A Dream

A girl called Louise, grew up wanting to become a professional footballer. This seemed like an impossible dream because Louise lived with her granny who believed that girls shouldn't play football. Louise wanted to prove her granny wrong in that girls can play football, so when she had her free time she would go out with her friends and practise her football skills. When she was walking home from school. Louise spotted a poster which read, 'Become a footballer today.'
Louise joined the football club where her skills were noticed by a professional footballer and her dreams came true.

Ebony Thompson (10)
Sugar Hill Primary School, Newton Aycliffe

The Dragon's Cave

She shouted, 'Help!' from inside the dragon's cave. The dragon roared and fire came from his mouth. The brave prince crossed the old bridge with his sword and shield in hand. 'I'm coming Princess Bella,' he shouted at the top of his voice. He got to the top entrance of the tunnel and there stood the huge red dragon. The dragon blew fire at him. The flames flew towards the prince. He held out his shield, the flames bounced off his shield and hit the dragon right in it's face, it flew off scared. The prince had saved his love.

Poppy Hobson (8)
Sugar Hill Primary School, Newton Aycliffe

Tiger Diaries!

Best Christmas ever! I got an adoption pack from London Zoo and I'm now the guardian of Jai-Jai the tiger! I can't wait to go and see him.

Today I met my tiger, Jai-Jai. He was a lot bigger in real life and had turquoise blue eyes. I was pleased there was glass between us though as he might have eaten me for lunch! I've just read my emails; Jai-Jai has a girlfriend called Malati and they've had two cubs called Rhubarb and Custard. I'm so happy as Sumatran tigers are endangered species.

Rhubarb and Custard rock!

Jude Hoar (10)
Sugar Hill Primary School, Newton Aycliffe

The Mummy Discovery!

Me and GMC were playing in my back garden. Suddenly I stood on a golden stone and it transported me back to ancient Egypt. I saw Tutankhamun and I saw Egyptians building a pyramid. Then an Egyptian girl came over and said, 'Would you like to go in one of the pyramids?' I said, 'Yes.' Then she took me and GMC to a pyramid. When we got inside we collected some jewels, suddenly a mummy woke up and started chasing us, so I stood on another golden stone. *Whoosh!* We were home safe and even kept the beautiful jewels.

Ruby Amelia Hindmarch (8)
Sugar Hill Primary School, Newton Aycliffe

Magic

Once when I was in the most magnificent magic show in the world! The magician did a few tricks, one was the box trick and guess what? I got to chop the magician in half! It should have been good right? No, in fact he turned into a venomous snake. 'What?' I said, Well I saw the wand in the tail so I tried to say 'Abracadabra' but it didn't work, so I then tried to say 'Abracados' but it didn't work. 'Argh!' After loads of magic words I tried 'Abracadabaz' and it worked, hooray!

Harry Laight (9)
Sugar Hill Primary School, Newton Aycliffe

Charlotte And The Squirrel

Charlotte was playing on her swing when she fell. When she opens her eyes, she was face to face with a squirrel who talked to her, asking her back for tea.

Charlotte went to the squirrel's tree house, on the table was a nut cake and chocolate milkshake. Charlotte took a bit of a scrumptious nut cake and to her surprise it started popping and fizzing in her mouth, she quickly took a drink of milkshake only to find the popping and bubbling got worse. She started laughing and giggling that much, she fell off her chair.

Jasmine Hope (9)
Sugar Hill Primary School, Newton Aycliffe

How Blackbeard Died

It was a beautiful day in North Carolina. It's a pity it's the last day I'll see, I Captain Will am hiding out here, having received the dreaded black spot from Edward Teach (Blackbeard). I've just found out he has tracked me down and is coming to kill me for selling him out to the British Navy. I run along the beach with him close behind! I can hear his angry shouts, 'At last you salty seadog, I have you,' he shouts.

'Saved.' The navy arrive, Teach is arrested. He will now be beheaded.

William Hall (10)
Sugar Hill Primary School, Newton Aycliffe

Evacuee

I pushed the palms of my hands onto the window pane as the train began to leave. I tried to keep Dad in sight for as long as I possibly could. A lump grew in my throat and a tear trickled down my cheek. I had to be strong for Tommy he was so young, I clenched his hand tight, 'We're going to be OK Tommy, the country is much safer for us.'
I looked out the window and everything I knew had vanished. An avalanche of emotions flowed over me, Tommy was the only familiar thing I had left.

Conner James Bennett (10)
Sugar Hill Primary School, Newton Aycliffe

Untitled

Dear Diary,

I was about to get eaten. I get some friends, then we went into a time machine. We went to the Cretaceous period, where I got separated from Dan, Drake and Roy. Then they ran in fear, that's when I saw the T-rex. He tried to eat me. Then I was back in normal time or so I thought.

Morgan Mason (9)
Sugar Hill Primary School, Newton Aycliffe

The Death Of Anne Boleyn

Henry VIII was the second Tudor monarch and well known for having six wives. Anne, Henry's second and most famous wife had a best friend called Isabelle. Anne told Isabelle her biggest secrets. Isabelle and Anne were inseparable. They both did everything together. Anne and Isabelle told each other stories of their life. They enjoyed walks around the gardens, sewing and tapestry. Isabelle came in crying one day because she overheard one of the guards speaking about, the death of the queen. On the day of Anne's death. She gave Isabelle her most prized possession, her mother's handkerchief.

Erin Russell (9)
Sugar Hill Primary School, Newton Aycliffe

The Mad Magician

Merlin the magician wears a long pointed hat, has a snowy white beard and clumsy hands and feet. Merlin's intention was to make the world with everybody in it to disappear. With a swish of his wand and his magical chant 'Alakazam hey presto,' the world was beginning to slowly disappear. People feared for their lives when he pointed his wand laughing mercilessly. Suddenly, Merlin tripped over his clumsy feet and his ancient wand zapped his old wrinkly face. Then, in a puff of smoke, he vanished into thin air still chanting, 'Alakazam all spam fritters, disappear horrible critters.'

Moore Swainston (7)
Sugar Hill Primary School, Newton Aycliffe

Saving Our Sister!

Alo and Chaska were woken late at night by the sounds of screaming and horses galloping. Frightened by the noises they quietly looked out of their wigwam to see horses being stolen along with their sister Aponi. Alo and Chaska were angry so got on their horses to chase after them. Being dark it was difficult weaving through the trees and rocks. Alo very quickly caught up with the thief and jumped on the back of his horse knocking him to the ground. Aponi climbed onto Chaska's horse then rounded up the horses and returned home! They got back home safely.

Anthony Gowland (9)
Sugar Hill Primary School, Newton Aycliffe

Untitled

As I entered the pitch-black darkness of the tomb, not knowing what awaited only having torch light to guide me. I walked deeper inside, admiring the hard carved hieroglyphics on the walls of the pyramid. The heat was unbearable until there it was right in front of my very own eyes. The sarcophagus of Tutankhamun. Made from solid gold just knowing what lay inside made my heart feel like it might burst out of my chest. His stuffed body wrapped in tight linen bandages surrounded by his prize possessions and riches all ready for his journey into the afterlife.

Alyisha Patton (9)
Sugar Hill Primary School, Newton Aycliffe

The Broken Moon Of Awe

The moon crescent crust of land, Santorini, was in a blaze, ruin and despair. Hephaestus was the first God there, not knowing the plan set up by Nemesis with help from the infamous Hades. Nemesis wanted revenge for what his old friend had done to him by stealing his lover Iris. As all the other gods arrived they instantly blamed Hephaestus for the damage done to the sacred stones of Santorini, but little did they know, a new source of power, evil and tyranny emerged. Death, destruction, decay in its purest form waiting to destroy the gods for all eternity.

Lexie Duffy (8)
Sugar Hill Primary School, Newton Aycliffe

Pirate Terror At Sea

The sun was settling behind a foggy mist, floating just above the Atlantic Ocean. The sound of the swooping waves was suddenly interrupted by a loud *boom!* A cannon has fired a blast that rocks the ship. Guns fire and flames flicker everywhere. The ship's wheel spins wildly as no one is steering. I sprinted to the wheel to save the lives of my crew but hooks have been fired and snarling men jump aboard. Pirates! Hissing through his teeth, one man stands tall, with pieces of rope burning in his hair. It was Blackbeard and his fierce crew...

Harvey Yale (8)
Sugar Hill Primary School, Newton Aycliffe

The Stone Age Begins

One morning there lived Mr and Mrs Kavanagh, they had a walk to the tallest mountain ever. They finally reached the top they glanced over and thought they had seen a Stone Age family. Mrs Kavanagh said to Mr Kavanagh, 'I just saw a Stone Age family!' They didn't know what to do so they went to sleep tossing and turning. They thought shall we ring the police. Finally said that they should ring the police. The police came to check if it was true. A few years later the police discovered that there was actually a family living there.

Lauren Kavanagh (8)
Sugar Hill Primary School, Newton Aycliffe

The Mummy Run!

It was Halloween, so my brother and I went to Egypt on holiday. We were taking photos of the tall pyramids, when all of a sudden we fell down a dark hole. We couldn't see anything but heard a loud groaning getting louder. We could see a white shadow in the distance coming towards us. So we started running. We kept running down the dark tunnels until we saw the daylight. The tall white shadows followed us into the daylight, they were mummies. One of them tripped over and came uncovered, it was actually my friends in a Halloween costume.

Tyler Cunliffe (9)
Sugar Hill Primary School, Newton Aycliffe

The Battle

It was a dark stormy night but John Jack and his troops were waiting to battle his enemy Albert Ball. As time went by John Jack and his troops prepared for battle. In the distance John Jack could hear loud booms and bangs which seemed to be getting closer. Without hesitation John Jack gave his troops the go-ahead to go into battle. The guns that were used by the troops were metallic black with sharp bayonets attached. The troops struck and won the battle for John Jack and his country. John Jack is still alive today to tell the tale.

Jack Surman (10)
Sugar Hill Primary School, Newton Aycliffe

The Victory!

It was a sunny Sunday morning and the team ready to play a match. Layton was the captain of his team and he was really excited. But the team that they were playing against were really hard. The first half went good it was a draw. In the second half the other team scored, Layton's team were worried. Then forty-five seconds to go, Thomas from Layton's team played the ball down the line for Joe, then Joe crossed it in for Layton and he scored the equaliser. It was penalty shootout time and we were victorious. We were the champions!

Layton Collier Grant (8)
Sugar Hill Primary School, Newton Aycliffe

Tasty Treats

The streets are littered with tasty treats. The smell is overpowering. I like it. I know if I can keep hidden the food around me will all be mine. It's 1665, plague is rife among the humans, dodging between the rubbish and tasty treats I see a horse and cart with a human yelling, 'Bring out your dead!' Houses are marked with a red cross, they either have it or died from it. I hear people saying we are the cause of the plague, we're not the ones to blame, humans leaving mess everywhere are, after all we're just rats!

Lucy Grayson (9)
Sugar Hill Primary School, Newton Aycliffe

Journey Of A Soul

Togo the pharaoh felt no more pain. He looked around, there was a huge golden gateway in the bright distance. The pharaoh walked towards it. As he approached he saw a snappy crocodile. She was huge and looked starving. Togo was at the gateway. Five gods appeared and one said, 'I am Atom, she is Sebmet, he is Bast, that is Horous and there is Geb.' Geb took Togo's heart from his dead body and put it on a gold scale. On the other side was a feather. The heart was lighter than the feather. Suddenly Tog's soul vanished.

Tyler Gibbon (9)
Sugar Hill Primary School, Newton Aycliffe

Nice Mummy After All

I was exploring a pyramid when suddenly I stumbled into a mysterious dark room. Just as I turned to leave. I smelt an horrific smell. My heart started to pound like a drum when I heard an unexplained creak. That's when I discovered a giant, rotten mummy creeping out of its ancient tomb. Petrified I ran for the exit with the mummy chasing after me. One skeleton finger popped out of its dusty bandages as it tried to grab me. I fell to my knees, instead of hurting me the mummy helped me up and explained he was just lonely.

Ellie Davies (9)
Sugar Hill Primary School, Newton Aycliffe

Dressing Me!

Once there was a young rich Roman lady called Rosetta who loved to call on her slave Lugassa to do everything she wanted. Rosetta lived in a beautiful villa with her husband Alfred, because they were rich, they wore different clothing to the other non rich Romans. Rosetta and her husband would call on their slave to dress them. Rosetta would wear a tunic with a dress and shawl over it and also have chalk on their face and paint her lips red. While her husband would dress in a tunic and have a toga wrapped over it.

Grace Buck (9)
Sugar Hill Primary School, Newton Aycliffe

The Mystery

The sandy desert of Egypt upon my feet with the sun blazing on my head. Looking around I saw sandy pyramids under the blue sky. Suddenly I saw something approaching me from behind the pyramids. I had no clue what it was. It dragged it's feet as it got closer. My heart froze, my feet stuck in place. I heard rustling as the mysterious figure was approaching. The sand started swirling and the figure slowly faded away then I heard a faint beeping and turned to find it was my alarm. I felt relieved it was all a dream.

Amy Richardson (8)
Sugar Hill Primary School, Newton Aycliffe

Anne's Diary, September 6th 1942

I am hiding, it is terrifying. I can hear voices. They are speaking in German. I must be quick or they will find me and my family. My heart races and I forget to breathe. I'm actually scared to breathe in case they can hear me. I hear footsteps getting closer. Can they hear my heart? It is thumping so loudly. The German soldiers are questioning our friends. The footsteps then fade, as do the voices, my heart slows, I can breathe again. My family and I embrace. My name is Anne Frank and I am thirteen years old.

Anna Wren (9)
Sugar Hill Primary School, Newton Aycliffe

Who's The Mummy?

I shouldn't have wandered away. Now I was hopelessly lost. Suddenly I heard an awful moaning sound that made my hair stand up on end. Hundreds of beetles ran past me. Then around the corner came a mummy, moving very fast for something so ancient. I ran as fast as I could and I fell over a fallen statue. I jumped up and started running again, I was scared stiff but I looked behind me. Luck was on my side, the bandages had caught on the statue and unwrapped. All that was left was a scary pile of twisted bones.

Sophie Grace Evans (9)
Sugar Hill Primary School, Newton Aycliffe

A Viking's Epic Journey

My name is Angry Bird. I'm a Viking travelling the North Sea heading to England ready to invade Britain. The waves were crashing, the boat was tossing to and fro, muscles aching and it felt like my back was breaking. This journey's taking forever. All of a sudden a dragon appeared it had eyes the colour of emeralds, razor-sharp teeth, thirty-four spikes on its head and neck and it was rustic red. So I got out my spear and slay the beast. So we continued our journey and finally Britain was coming upon us.

Callum McBride (9)
Sugar Hill Primary School, Newton Aycliffe

The Monster Story

It was late at night, I was asleep in my bed. Sparkles, twinkled all around a wild wind swept me up. I landed in a pile of twigs and leaves. There were huge eggs around me. I was squashed in-between them. I could hear the squawks of the mummy pterodactyl coming! She swooped through the air, beating her enormous wings, getting closer, I was frightened! I scrambled my way through the nest and peeped over the top. It was a long way down to the rocky ground. One big jump to safety and I landed back in my warm bed.

Keira Richardson (9)
Sugar Hill Primary School, Newton Aycliffe

Holiday In Egypt

On holiday in Egypt, Wayne and I decided to visit the deserts. When suddenly out the corner of my eye I saw a big shadow appear. My heart froze I shouted with all my might, 'Run Wayne.' Wayne then quickly turned around to see a mummy was travelling so close towards us, but had nowhere to run or hide. Our legs froze, sweat dripping off my forehead. We dropped to our knees. I thought I was going to die. I then saw a thread so I sharply pulled it away from the mummy, to our surprise it was my grandad!

Alfie Land (8)
Sugar Hill Primary School, Newton Aycliffe

Anne Boleyn

Today is the 19th May 1536. I am up for execution, the guards show me the way to Tower Green within the walls of the Tower of London. I'm ordered to climb the scaffold where a French swordsman is waiting. Praying that Henry VIII changes his mind, I declare my love for him. The swordsman tells me to kneel down. The audience look terrified and you can hear a pin drop. My heart is beating fast and my hands are shaking. As I kneel the guardsman raises his sword. I close my eyes and take a deep breath...

Sophie Flint (9)
Sugar Hill Primary School, Newton Aycliffe

The Huge Rescue

It is so cold, I felt exhausted. The sea was rough and the winds were blowing sea water in my eyes. I could see the large rocks up ahead. Nine people were clinging to rocks for their lives. Dad got off the boat to help them, leaving me to control the boat. I was terrified, the winds would crash my boat into the rocks. I managed to stay strong and remembered everything Dad told me. My arms were aching but I persevered. All nine people were saved that day. My name is Grace Darling and I am a big heroine.

Joe Wren (8)
Sugar Hill Primary School, Newton Aycliffe

Hungry Henry

Once there was a cook, Henry VIII's cook. His name was George and he had to get up really early every morning to make Henry's breakfast. Henry liked a huge plate of roast chicken and a large amount of chocolate chip cupcakes. Usually he ate the lot and the only thing he left were the bones that he sucked clean. Not only did he have breakfast but he also had brunch, lunch, afternoon tea, supper and a bedtime snack to finish. No wonder Henry was fat, and no wonder George was so tired.

Oliver Paylor (8)
Sugar Hill Primary School, Newton Aycliffe

The Return Of The Pyramids

It was a cold, foggy day as I came to the pyramid entrance. I could hear banging coming from inside the dark creepy tunnel. There was a torch burning bright at the dark entrance. I grabbed hold of it and made my way down the dark tunnel. *Bang! Bang!* I heard it again. I knew I had to see where the noise was, as I came to the end of the dark, creepy tunnel I could see a brightly coloured tomb. I opened it and something creepy grabbed my arm, I screamed and ran for my life, I'm scared.

Isaac Taylor (9)
Sugar Hill Primary School, Newton Aycliffe

Mummy Attack!

One day an Egyptian, Abdul, went to meet his friend called Bob then he heard a sound, a mysterious sound, a sound he had never heard before. But Bob never heard the sound before either. Then they saw a pyramid and read what it said: 'You will get chased in ten seconds and a mummy will come and attack you to death and crush your bones. You will be dead forever and ever until you're a mummy'. But Bob thought it wasn't real but Abdul thought it was real. The mummy came after them.

Ruby Hancock (8)
Sugar Hill Primary School, Newton Aycliffe

Shootout

As a stranger rode into High Chaparral. Women, children and men ran into their houses full of fear in the town as the streets went quiet. I knew that I Sheriff Bick would have to face evil Ramsey in a shootout, man on man. I walked and stood in the middle of the street facing him, we stood, looked and waited. His hand twitched, he went for his gun, I went for mine, shots rang out. I fell to the ground with pain in my leg. I looked up and Ramsey was down not moving, just bleeding out.

Chloe Heslop (9)
Sugar Hill Primary School, Newton Aycliffe

The Wolf Deaths

It's a boy and a wolf, there's metal pegs on the trees the boy climbs it and the wolf does. They both go on a bendy branch then it snaps. I was strolling through the woods then heard a howling growling fierce wolf back through there were metal pegs on the trees. I climbed one, I got up but the wolf got close. I got up I went across the bendy branch, it came then I struggled then the branch fell off in a flash. I was dead in the deep dark woods all frosty and leaves all over.

Rhys Galloway (9)
Sugar Hill Primary School, Newton Aycliffe

Liam The Caveman

One stormy day I left my cave for an adventure. I went into the forest with my spear hunting for food. Suddenly I heard something growling at me, I was shivering with fear. It sounded like it was right in front of me so I put my spear ahead of me as I went forward it was getting louder and louder! It stopped a tiger sprinted towards me. As the tiger was running it tripped and hurt its leg and I stabbed it. I took the meat and ran off. On my way home I saw Thug, my best friend.

Liam Bell (9)
Sugar Hill Primary School, Newton Aycliffe

The Dragon Demon

Jack was walking into a huge cave in Wales. Suddenly he saw a purple skinned dragon! The dragon was going to kill Jack! Jack screamed, 'Argh!' He tried to run away but the dragon zoomed to the entrance and blocked him. Jack felt anxious. Then Jack remembered he had his bow and arrow and shot the vicious dragon right in the eye. The dragon fell to the ground. It was dead! Jack ran over to the dragon and stabbed him with his ultimate shiny sword and then headed back to camp.

Thomas Aspinall (9)
Sugar Hill Primary School, Newton Aycliffe

The Battle Of Billy Smith

My name is Billy Smith and I fought beside my brother, Fred Smith, at the Battle of the Somme in 1916. The battle lasted a total of one hundred and forty one days. The first day of the battle was on the 1st of July1916. My brother Fred and I waited in a trench for the signal to attack the enemy. The whistles blew and we began to advance. A shell exploded near us and Fred was hit. I carried him to a medic through gunfire. Fred survived and we both lived to tell the tale.

Harry Surman (8)
Sugar Hill Primary School, Newton Aycliffe

He's Real!

It was a cold, frosty night and the moon was high in the sky. Suddenly I saw something in the corner of my eye. As it approached I noticed a long, ginger beard that hung from its shelf like chin. It hung from its chin like a red waterfall. Its hair was long, ginger and greasy. All of a sudden it began to run towards me. As it was pointing its double-sided axe at me, naturally I ran for my life. 'You coward,' it shouted. When I turned around I realised it was Thor...

Michael Pritchard (9)
Sugar Hill Primary School, Newton Aycliffe

The Lonely Soldier

It was cold and wet, all alone in the mud down in a ditch. The sound of gunfire and the smell of smoke. No one to help me they were all gone. So I kept cover as gunshots flew through the air, praying to God that I would be OK. As time went by it all went quiet so I peeped out the trench to find no one was there. Then in the trees I heard a whisper, gun at the ready I crept quickly to find my sergeant who took me to safety. Sticking together is always better.

Teegan Briscoe (8)
Sugar Hill Primary School, Newton Aycliffe

Dad The Zombie

One day I was at the shops looking for clothes, I saw lots of T-shirts with zombies on them. So I bought one! After I got served I decided to go home because it was getting late. When I got home I heard a creaking noise? But I just went to bed. While I was sleeping, I felt a huge shadow above me I woke up in a fright! I saw a zombie! Well I thought it was a zombie, but in fact it was my dad coming in to check on me.

Gracie-Mai Cowper (8)
Sugar Hill Primary School, Newton Aycliffe

The Scary Volcano

Debra, Peter and Charlie were having dinner when the room started shaking wildly. Peter looked outside and the amazing and scary volcano in Pompeii was erupting! Quickly Debra and Peter got a boat into the water and put the wooden oars onto the boat. Peter stepped in and tested it to see if it worked correctly. It worked, so in went Charlie and then Debra who came in last and happily they sailed in the boat away.

Sophie M (9)
Sugar Hill Primary School, Newton Aycliffe

The End Of The Dinos!

Here our heroic story begins! There was a little boy who was very intelligent and cool, his name was James. He wished he could see the meteor hit the dinosaurs, so he built a time machine and went back, but he fell onto a dinosaur back and it broke! So he defeated the mean dinosaur with the caveman's help! He rebuilt the time machine and went back to now! 'It's good to be home!' he said.

James Behan (9)
Sugar Hill Primary School, Newton Aycliffe

The Beasts Are Gobbling!

The wind whistled, trees rustle and the river splashed as the rocks tumbled into the river. Just then banging started, it got louder and louder it saw me, so I ran, it was really fast. It pulled trees from the ground. It crunched as the monster ate the tree. They had me cornered up against a fence. It roared. It had razor-sharp teeth. It had four legs. It had orange and black stripe on it.

Lincoln Hudson (8)
Sugar Hill Primary School, Newton Aycliffe

Farmers Became Vikings

I didn't want to work on my brother's farm. I wanted fame and fortune for myself. So I set sail from my home town of Scandinavia and headed towards England. I will trade, raid and plunder from other countries. I trade iron for wheat and silver with Britain and timber and fur for gold and wine from the Mediterranean. I wear wolf skin and howl in battle. I am called Berserber.

Ryan Foreman (9)
Sugar Hill Primary School, Newton Aycliffe

The Mummy's Coming

A long time ago a little boy opened a pyramid, in there was a mummy, it was wrapped in bandages, he looked at it and he ran away. The next day he returned and cut off the bandages. The mummy began to move the boy ran away and he told the police what he had done. The mummy was captured outside the pyramid he was taken back and the tomb was sealed never to be opened again.

Ellie Horner (7)
Sugar Hill Primary School, Newton Aycliffe

The Dragon Chase

The grass stood on end, as the wind howled and the trees toppled over and the monster rose from the ground. I stumbled over and I stood up gripping my hands up a tree trunk and ran for my life, the mind was slapping of my face. The beast almost got me. Suddenly I could not run any further. It was a dragon!

Lydia Deboer (8)
Sugar Hill Primary School, Newton Aycliffe

What Is Behind The Sand?

I walked in the soft, yellow sand. The sand felt as soft as a lolly. The wind howled like a wolf. Suddenly I saw something. It was white, long and thin. It walked very strangely! Then a sandstorm came. What is the thing behind the sand? I stepped back! In a blink I saw what it was... a mummy.

Emma Ainsworth (10)
Sugar Hill Primary School, Newton Aycliffe

Years of YoungWriters

YOUNG WRITERS
INFORMATION

We hope you have enjoyed reading this book – and that you will continue to in the coming years.

If you're a young writer who enjoys reading and creative writing, or the parent of an enthusiastic poet or story writer, do visit our website www.youngwriters.co.uk. Here you will find free competitions, workshops and games, as well as recommended reads, a poetry glossary and our blog.

If you would like to order further copies of this book, or any of our other titles give us a call or visit **www.youngwriters.co.uk**.

'HE CAME, HE SAW, HE CONKED US'!

Young Writers
Remus House
Coltsfoot Drive
Peterborough
PE2 9BF

(01733) 890066
info@youngwriters.co.uk

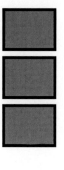

XEROX

Hot Folder User

Document Name: YB0292G – AA – Hampshire Tales.pdf
Printing Time: 01/25/17 18:02:02
Copies Requested: 4
Account:
Virtual Printer: Nuvera2/YB–A4
Printed For: